MEG'S EGGS

for Katie

MEG'S EGGS

by Helen Nicoll
and Jan Pieńkowski

PUFFIN BOOKS

It was suppertime, so Meg got out her cauldron

I'm hungry

Where's my egg?

She
put
in

lizards, newts, 2 green frogs

They could not break the eggs

supper

any

without

to bed

went

and

In the
middle
of the
night
Meg
heard

Meg's egg was hatching

Meg took Diplodocus to

the pond

Diplodocus was very happy

Mog was sleeping by his egg

when he heard a noise

Mog
took
Stegosaurus
into
the
garden

Owl
was
watching
the
last
egg

Out jumped Tyrannosaurus, the most ferocious of all the dinosaurs

They
were
very
frightened

Meg flew home and tried
to make a good spell

Goodbye!